The Midnight Panda

Look out for more books by Holly Webb

www.holly-webb.com

The Midnight Panda

HOLLY WEBB

Illustrated by Sharon Rentta

SCHOLASTIC

First published in the UK in 2016 by Scholastic Children's Books
An imprint of Scholastic Ltd
Euston House, 24 Eversholt Street
London, NW1 1DB, UK
Registered office: Westfield Road, Southam, Warwickshire, CV47 0RA
SCHOLASTIC and associated logos are trademarks and/
or registered trademarks of Scholastic Inc.

Text copyright © Holly Webb, 2016
Illustration copyright © Sharon Rentta, 2016

The rights of Holly Webb and Sharon Rentta to be identified as the author
and illustrator of this work have been asserted by them.
Cover illustration © Sharon Rentta, 2016

ISBN 978 1407 14487 0

A CIP catalogue record for this book is available from the British Library.

Printed by CPI Group (UK) Ltd, Croydon, CR0 4YY
Papers used by Scholastic Children's Books are made
from wood grown in sustainable forests.

1 3 5 7 9 10 8 6 4 2

www.scholastic.co.uk
www.holly-webb.com

For Robin

1

James struggled up out of a strange, bright dream world, swimming past sharks, and jellyfish with long, poison-suckered tentacles. He shot up in bed, pressing himself desperately against the wooden headboard, gasping for breath. If he could breathe, it must only have been a dream. No one could breathe underwater, so it was a dream; it wasn't real. It didn't mean anything.

He curled up into the corner of the bed against the wall, hauling his duvet up around his shoulders, his breath still shuddering in and out. He could see tentacles, thin and deadly,

1

flickering around the corners of his eyes. He peered into the darkness of his bedroom, the rags of the dream fluttering around him. They were fading now, though. He was almost sure that he was safe.

Except that it was so dark. It must be the middle of the night. He couldn't hear anything at all from downstairs, no talking, no television. No music from Anna's room. Everyone was asleep. He was all alone in the dark, and it was nearly midnight. James wriggled further back into the wall, and felt his breaths get faster again, in and out. The dark was all round him. He was even breathing the dark. If he was breathing it in, then it knew he was there. The dark could see him.

"You're being stupid," James whispered to

himself. He tried to say it louder, really loud, but a whisper was all that he could manage. His voice just wouldn't come out any bigger. The dark was pressing it back inside him, like a great, soft hand stopping up his mouth. "Go back to sleep," James whispered to himself. "It's easy."

But it wasn't. He felt horribly awake, the blood racing round his body, his thoughts jumping and snapping. He wasn't sleepy at all.

James had been scared of the dark for as long as he could remember. He didn't know why, or how it had started. He just hated the feeling of the darkness all around him, settling on his skin. Mum always left the landing light on for him at bedtime – but now she and Dad had gone to bed, and all the lights were off. He didn't even have a street lamp shining through the window, since his room looked out on to the garden. It had to be really late. James peered at the luminous hands on his clock. It looked odd, as though it was broken – until he realized that both the hands were in a straight line pointing up. It was midnight. The darkest, strangest, scariest part of the night.

He stared out at his room, his eyes fighting with the shadows, trying to work out what all these odd, lumping midnight shapes must be. His bedside table, with a water bottle and a pile of books. The chair in front of his desk. The wardrobe, huge and hulking in the corner. And behind the wardrobe, by the door, growing gradually clearer as his eyes got used to the darkness, was a tall figure. James gulped, his fingers tensing on the edge of his duvet. The figure loomed out from the space between the wardrobe and the door, its fur showing as vague patches of light and dark in the shadows. It was clear, though, what it was.

A bear. Standing in the corner by his wardrobe, and staring at him. A huge bear. In his bedroom.

Was he dreaming again? James screwed his eyes tight shut, hoping that when he opened them again the bear would have disappeared. But it hadn't. It was still there, and it even seemed to be reaching out towards him. Could it see him? Did it know he was there? James peered sideways at the switch for his bedside light, as far as he could without moving. It made his eyes hurt, straining them sideways like that,

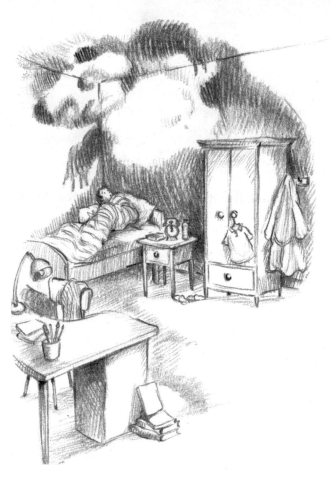

but he didn't care. If he moved, the bear might pounce. Bears were big, but they were fast; he'd watched enough wildlife programmes to know that. That bear could scoop him out of bed in a flash, just like it would snatch a silvery fish out of a river. He wouldn't even have time to wriggle.

Thinking about it, there was no way he could get to the light switch, not without alerting the bear. He'd just have to stay there and hope it went away.

Where could it have come from, anyway? In the dark, a hundred wild ideas went flashing past James's eyes. A circus? A zoo? It couldn't be an escaped pet; it was just too big. For a second a picture flitted into his head of the bear on a lead, and then curling up in a basket.

But then James peered back through the shadows at the size of the thing, and the comforting picture faded. That bear would never fit in a basket. It would take up all of the sofa downstairs, and then some.

James worm-wriggled himself sideways, millimetre by millimetre, flinching as his duvet rustled – he froze, waiting for the bear to leap across the room. But it stayed, staring out into the shadows. Perhaps it was far enough away not to hear? James took a deeper, slower breath, and pressed his cheek against the wall.

"Anna!" he whispered. "Anna, help! There's a great big bear in my bedroom. Come and help! You have to help me chase it away...!" But there was no answering whisper. James flicked an anxious glance towards the bear again – still there, still still – and whispered louder. "Anna! Anna, please don't be asleep..." She couldn't be. Anna swore to him that she never, ever slept at all, and it was true that she never seemed to be asleep if he went into to her room at night. She was always listening to music or messaging her friends. She was only asleep in the mornings when Mum was trying to get her out of bed for school.

The bear was right next to his bedroom door, James thought suddenly. If Anna came through the door, the bear would probably be furious and eat his big sister first. James squashed down the sudden skip his heart made, and scowled at himself. "But don't just come in my room," he whispered on urgently. "He's right by the door. I mean – maybe it isn't a bear, but there's this thing. . ." Anna would never believe it was really a bear, would she? James could hardly believe it himself. He was too old to believe in stuff like this – monsters under the bed. "I don't know what it is, but it's something, Anna. Tell Dad. Or Mum. Or do something. Please!"

The bear still hadn't moved, and James's voice was starting to hurt from all the strangled whispering. There was no sound from next door. He tapped his fingernails lightly against the wall, and then again. No answer. She was asleep after all, and that meant he was all alone – with the bear.

Hopeless, James slid down further under the duvet, so that his face was covered. It was warm and airless and even darker under there, but he couldn't see the bear, and there was hardly any room for dark, really, with the way the duvet clung round him. He cupped one hand over his nose to make a space to breathe in, and closed his eyes, waiting to be eaten.

2

James woke up smothered and hot under his duvet, but he was pretty sure that he hadn't been eaten. He was definitely still alive. So that was good. Cautiously, he pulled back the clinging duvet and peered over the top.

No bear. Not even a sign of one. He sat up, and then crawled to the end of his bed to look properly at the gap beside the wardrobe. James knelt at the end of the bed – he felt safer there, as if the bed were an island in a stormy sea, one with bears swimming about in it. The bear seemed to have gone, but who knew for certain? His bedroom felt so different in daylight, though. It was hard to believe he'd been so scared the night before. Perhaps it had just been a really weird nightmare, and he'd never even woken up?

"Are you getting up?" His mum put her head round the door and smiled at him. Then she noticed his strange pose, balanced on the edge of the mattress. "Have you lost something?" She bent over, trying to see whatever it was he was looking for under his bed. "Oh, James, how much grot are you hiding under there? It's horrible. Is that an apple core?"

James ignored her. She wasn't going to listen to whatever excuses he made – he'd been at a really good bit in his book, and it was just simpler to drop the apple there than get up and go to the bin – and all he really needed to do was let her tell him off and then say he was sorry, and that he'd never, ever do it again. Besides, what was really important was that his mum was standing right next to where the bear had been, and she didn't seem to have noticed two metres of lethal furry animal standing next to her. It hadn't bitten a lump out of her yet, either.

So it was gone. Or it had never been there at all. He let out a slow breath of relief, and then tried to look apologetic for his mum. "I'll pick it up, Mum, and that apple's not really messy anyway, I think it's mummified, look. . ."

The fact that he hadn't been eaten by a bear made even a long, dull Monday morning lesson on fractions seem bearable. James kept taking deep, slow breaths of relief as he remembered all over again that it had just been a weird dream. He found that he was looking at his hands, spread out on the table in front of him. All there, every finger! Not eaten! He'd never noticed how much he loved his fingers before. James plaited them together, and smirked at them. Just a dream, even if it had felt so real last night. How could he really have thought there was a bear in his bedroom? It wasn't as if there were bears anywhere round here, was it? What were they doing, living in the woods down by the lake? Where Dad took him to ride his bike? James shook his head very slightly. "Stupid," he mouthed to himself.

"I'd forgotten it was this Friday!" James's friend Evan nudged him.

"What is?" James blinked, holding his side. Evan's elbows were pointy.

"Do you never listen?"

James blinked again. Evan sounded just like his mother.

"The trip! To the museum! The sleepover! Wake up, James!" Evan rolled his eyes and grinned at him.

"Oh..." They weren't still talking about fractions, then. James actually looked at the whiteboard, instead of staring through it into a wood full of bears chasing boys on bikes, and saw that Miss Morley had put up a picture of the museum gallery.

She was beaming round at all of them. "Now, I'm not sure exactly where our group will get to sleep – there are other schools going too – but it'll be somewhere in one of the natural-history galleries. We could be sleeping next to a stuffed lion! Or under a case full of spiders!"

A few people made "Ooooh, I'm scared!" noises, and Elise went white. "Spiders? We won't really have to sleep by spiders, will we, Miss Morley? I hate them."

"Baby!" hissed one of the boys on her table, and Elise looked down at her book miserably.

"Be quiet, Kai," Miss Morley said firmly. "I'm sure we can put you well away from anything like that, Elise, don't worry."

"My brother's got a tarantula," one of the other boys boasted. "He says I can bring it in for show-and-tell."

"Absolutely not," Miss Morley snapped, and Elise shrank down in her chair as Kai walked his fingers across the table towards her, tarantula-style.

Evan shook his head and sighed. "Freddy and Kai are such a pain," he muttered. "They have to show off about everything. Mind you, Elise could try being a bit less of a wimp. She's scared of everything."

James nodded, but his mind was racing. He hadn't thought of it before – he'd just been excited at the idea of a trip, and missing an afternoon of school, and general coolness. But how dark would a museum be at night?

And did a natural-history gallery have bears?

James was in goal at break time, but the football game had stalled. Kai said Freddy had slammed into him on purpose, and Freddy swore he hadn't, and even if he had it was Kai's fault because Kai was cheating, and anyway it was his ball, so what he said went. Now one of the lunchtime controllers was trying to sort it out, but she wasn't getting anywhere. James was fairly sure she was going to give up and ban them all from playing anyway. He sighed and sat down on the wall, between the chalked-on goalposts. It was just typical that Freddy and Kai had to ruin football today. He needed something to stop him thinking about the dark. And bears.

All the way through the football game (it hadn't been very good, even before Kai and Freddy got going) James had been wondering if the bear in his room had been a dream after all. It hadn't felt like a dream – he was almost sure he had woken up; he remembered looking at his clock and thinking the hands were broken.

All this was taking a while to think out, because he was sleepy from being awake so much of the night before. His thoughts were swirling round and round in a sort of thick, slow soup. He was getting towards the answer, though, and he didn't like it at all.

He knew there was no way the bear had been real. There wasn't a zoo anywhere near – no nearer than London, he was pretty sure. And he hadn't seen a poster for a circus. Circuses weren't even allowed to have bears any more, because it was cruel. James sort of agreed with that, but right now he wasn't really on the bears' side.

So, not a real bear.

That wasn't making James feel better, though. Because if it wasn't a real live bear, it was probably a dead one, he reckoned. Or a never-alive one. A sort of ghost bear. A monster, like all those other weird monsters that he'd seen in the dark, or heard scuffling around under his bed. But worse. And scarier. None of the others had ever really been anything – just DARK. But the bear had looked exactly like a bear. It made him feel shivery just to think of it.

Being out in the bright sun of the playground helped a bit, but not enough. What would happen that night, when it got dark, just a bit later than bedtime? If he wasn't safely asleep, would the bear turn up again? Where was it now? Perhaps it lived behind his wardrobe – it would be nice and shadowy there, even in the daytime, and a nightmare-bear could fit easily where a real bear couldn't.

It was going to come back. He'd been so happy that morning, when he woke and there was nothing there, but that didn't mean anything. The sun had been shining in under his curtains by the time Mum had woken him, so the bear must have sneaked back to its daytime lair. As soon as the night grew dark, it would squeeze out again, and sharpen its claws on the side of his wardrobe.

James shuddered. "You don't know that!" he whispered to himself fiercely. "Shut up!"

"Me?" a hurt voice asked, from somewhere up above, and James turned round sharply, grazing the backs of his legs on the bricks.

Elise was sitting on the sloping grass bank behind him, making daisy chains. They were drooping from her hands now as she stared at him.

"Um, no. I didn't mean you. I was just talking to myself."

Telling myself to shut up. That sounds so stupid.

"Oh." Elise only nodded. "I do that too," she said, looking back down at her daisies. "Sometimes it helps, doesn't it?"

"It helps. . . ?" James gaped at her.

"If I'm getting scared about stuff." She glanced at him for a second. "It's almost like somebody else saying it's going to be OK. . ." Elise folded her lips tightly, and randomly grabbed a couple of daisies. She'd picked them too short, James could tell. He waited for her to go on, but she didn't, and he realized that her cheeks were going red. She probably wished she hadn't said anything now, he thought.

"Yeah," he muttered gruffly. "I was doing that. I don't think it is going to be OK, though," he added, before he could stop himself. If that bear in the dark was all something he'd made up, he ought not to be scared of it, but he was. And if he'd made it up, then maybe it wouldn't just be in his bedroom – it could be anywhere. Even on a school trip, where everyone could see how frightened he was.

Elise looked at him, and he thought she wanted to tell him something, but then she just nodded again – and the bell went, and she hopped down from the bank and went running back into school.

James followed her slowly, wondering what it was she'd been trying to say. She was scared of things too – spiders, and dogs, and probably loads of other stuff. He'd seen her cry because Lucy's mum had brought their dog to pick Lucy up from school. Dogs weren't allowed in the playground, so Lucy's mum was waiting by the gate, and the dog had sniffed at Elise as she walked past. Elise practically collapsed in a heap.

Maybe Elise was scared of the dark as well? James watched her dash through the door. The thing was, he'd laughed at her a bit, with Evan and the others. But if his friends knew that he was scared of the dark, they'd laugh at him too.

James clenched his fists tightly inside his pockets, so tight that he could feel his fingernails digging into his skin. He wasn't sure whether he was more afraid of the dark – and whatever it was that was hiding in it – or of everyone thinking he was a baby.

3

James looked cautiously around his bedroom. He'd avoided coming upstairs since he came back from school. He'd done his homework at the kitchen table, saying it was tricky and he needed help, and then pleaded with Mum for some PlayStation time after dinner. But he couldn't put bedtime off any longer.

It was still quite light, the evening sun golden and warm. But James felt shivery. It was the way he had to keep turning round, to check there wasn't anything behind him.

Would the bear come back? James had a horrible sense that he wasn't alone. That something was waiting for him. The shadows around the wardrobe looked darker than they ought to be, thick and treacle-sticky. He had left the door open, and the space out on the landing was warmer and softer and more welcoming than the shadows of his room. James longed to go back out there – but how could he explain to Mum and Dad that he wanted to sleep on the landing instead of in his own bedroom? They knew he was scared of the dark, but James was sure that they didn't know what it really felt like. Mum had promised him that he'd grow out of it, and not to worry. But how was he supposed to stop himself worrying? He couldn't just turn worrying off.

James put his pyjamas on, occasionally whirling round to check that he wasn't being crept up on. Then he stood looking at his bed. He wasn't getting in it. He hadn't quite got as far as saying that to himself until now, but he was sure. He couldn't. What if he had to lie there for hours like he had last night? Watching the bear as the bear watched him? It had felt like hours, anyway.

The light was fading now. James could almost see the shadows, creeping further out from under his bed and behind the wardrobe. He picked up the fleecy blanket from the end of his bed and wrapped it round his shoulders like a cloak, sinking his chin down underneath the folds, so the dark couldn't get at him. He stared fixedly at the wardrobe, but there was no bear. Not yet.

Something rustled outside his window, and

James jumped round, his heart hammering. Just a bird. Or perhaps next door's cat. James turned away, shivering a little, and then gasped as a huge, shadowy thing loomed out for a second between his wardrobe and the door. The bear!

It was gone almost as quickly as it had appeared, but James knew it would be back – and that he couldn't stand being in his room, waiting.

He wouldn't do it! He didn't have to... Mum and Dad thought he was in bed, so that was OK. He would just sleep somewhere else. Somewhere really safe, away from bears.

James's feet had decided where he was going before he even thought of it. He was already hurrying along the landing and into Anna's room when he understood. Anna was the bravest person he knew. She wasn't scared of big dogs (it was a favourite family story that she had disappeared during a barbecue at Uncle Jake's house and been found trying to ride his huge Dobermann like a pony). She actually quite liked spiders. She always volunteered to be the one to rescue them with a jam jar and a bit of cardboard, and she talked to them lovingly as she took them outside to the garden, telling them how much nicer it was outside, and how sorry she was if the spider had been upset by Mum screaming, and that she would never, ever let Mum suck them up with the vacuum cleaner, like she threatened she would.

The only thing Anna was scared of was eggs – she said they were weird and wobbly and she wasn't eating anything that came out of a chicken's bum anyway. But she made an exception for cake – if she couldn't see the egg, she didn't mind pretending it wasn't there.

James would sleep in Anna's room, and she could protect him from the bear. She would probably thump it over the head with a book and tell it to get lost. James trotted into her room, feeling hugely relieved. Anna would understand about the bear – he should have told her about it as soon as they got home from school. In fact, she'd probably have been able to get rid of it straight away. She'd probably tease him a bit – but she did that all the time anyway. James wouldn't mind if she laughed at him, as long as she chased away the bear. He was just starting to tell Anna that he'd been stupid, and he needed her help, when he realized she wasn't actually there.

She was at swimming club. James sat down on her bed with a huff. He'd forgotten. Anna wouldn't be back for ages. And he was so tired. He couldn't stay up until she got back and explain it all then, he just couldn't. He looked enviously at Anna's warm, comfortable bed, beautifully free of bears, and thought about just getting in it. Except if Anna walked in and found him in her bed, she'd make a great fuss, and Mum would send him back to his own room. And Anna would be coming home just when it was getting dark, and ghost bears were properly coming out. No. He couldn't let her. It wouldn't be enough even to write a note, James thought, looking around the room anxiously. There was nothing to say that Anna would read it before she turfed him out of her bed. It was too risky.

Anna's bed was a cabin bed, with a desk that stuck out of the side of it, and storage boxes and bags of old clothes and her sleeping bag and all sorts of other stuff underneath. There were even some floor cushions, from when Anna decided to make it into a den. James sighed with happiness and crawled into the dim little space, laying out the cushions and pulling Anna's sleeping bag over himself. It was perfect. He would be quite safe from bears overnight with Anna there. If a bear turned up, Anna would chase it away, and if it didn't, he'd just explain to Anna in the morning why he was under her bed.

He huddled the sleeping bag up around

his ears, and it was as if sleep came with it, wrapping him in a soft cocoon of warmth. James didn't wake at all when Anna banged open the door and flung down her swimming bag and clattered around the room getting ready for bed. He slept on, warm and safe and certain that no ghost bear would dare raise a paw against his sister.

Faintly, in his dreams – warm, comfortable dreams of school and holidays and good things, the sort of dreams he could never quite remember properly when he woke up – James heard voices. It was the strange high note of worry in them that came whistling through his dreams.

"Is he in your room? You know, if he had a nightmare and woke up and went to find you. Maybe he's asleep in your bed."

That was Anna. And Dad was answering her. "I hadn't thought of that!" And then, from further away: "No, he isn't! James! James, where are you?"

"You don't think he's been sleepwalking?" Mum sounded as though she was standing right next to Anna's bed.

"No, it was Anna who used to do that."

"But that doesn't mean James couldn't have started to do it too. He does dream – he tells me his nightmares sometimes; they're so real-sounding. I wouldn't be surprised if he could walk in some of them. What if he's gone out?"

"I was downstairs in the living room, Jo; he couldn't have opened the front door without me hearing him. I promise."

"Where is he, then?" Mum's voice was so panicked that James rolled over in his sleep, slid off the cushions and banged his head against the back of Anna's desk. He whimpered, feeling for the bump and finding a slim bruised groove in his forehead.

"Did you hear?"

"Where is he?"

"Was that him?"

"He's under my bed! James, get out of there!"

"Hang on, Anna, I think he's still half asleep. James, come here, come on, it's OK." Dad was hauling him out, still in a bundle of sleeping bag and cushions. "What were you doing under there, James? We didn't know where you were. We were really worried."

"I banged my head. . ."

"It's all right, it's just a bit of a bump," Dad said soothingly. "But why were you under Anna's bed? It's ten o'clock, you should have been asleep ages ago. In your bed, not Anna's.

"There was a bear. . ." James said wearily. He couldn't explain. Dad would laugh. And Dad was carrying him back to his own room, and it was dark. James buried his face in Dad's shoulder, almost certain that he'd feel claws slash down his back as they went past the wardrobe. But there was nothing. Not even a growl.

"Don't go!" he whispered urgently, as his dad tipped him back into his own bed and wriggled him out of Anna's sleeping bag. "Don't leave me here with the bear. . ."

Dad laughed. "You're still asleep, aren't you? Maybe Mum's right, and you were sleepwalking."

"Please don't go." James peered round his dad's back. There was a thick, shadowy bulk looming out around the edge of the wardrobe. The bear was there, watching them. "Please!"

"All right, all right. . ." His dad's voice was soft and soothing, the sort of voice especially for a child who was having a nightmare, or a tantrum. He didn't understand. He didn't know that the bear was so much more than that.

"Don't leave me alone," James whispered, clinging to his dad's arm. "Not till I'm asleep."

His dad sighed and lay down beside him, warm and big and smelling of spaghetti bolognese because he'd cooked the dinner. It was enormously comforting. James turned his face into his dad's sleeve, and refused to look at the bear. It might be that if he wasn't looking, it wasn't there anyway. He didn't know.

4

"But James, you must have been under Anna's bed for a reason." Mum was using her best calm voice, which made James feel all scratchy. She ran her hands through her hair and stared down at James, who was stirring his cereal. "Please just eat your breakfast, love!"

James let go of the spoon and sat with his hands in his lap, head hanging.

Mum sighed. "Look, I'm sorry, James. Everyone's tired. Dad and I were really worried about you last night. We spent a long while looking for you."

Anna turned round from the toaster. "It took

me ages to get to sleep," she said, waving a piece of toast at him. "It's creepy, having you hiding under my bed."

Creepy! James thought. *I'm the one with a massive evil bear living behind my wardrobe! You don't know anything about creepy!* "I wasn't hiding," he muttered.

"Yes, you were!" Anna started buttering her toast. "And hurry up with your cereal, you'll make us late."

All thoughts of telling Anna about the bear and asking for her help died away to nothing. Last night he had been so sure that she would protect him from the bear, but now she was in her cool-big-sister mode, where it wasn't any use asking her for things. Today would be the kind of day when she wouldn't even wave to him as she walked past his school.

"James, you must know why you were there," Mum said gently, crouching down by his chair and staring at him. "Was something wrong? Was it one of those bad nightmares? We can't help if you don't tell us. . ."

"You did spook us all a bit," Dad said, smiling.

"I didn't mean to." It was sort of true. He had meant to sleep under Anna's bed, but he hadn't meant to upset everybody. He hadn't meant to be found.

"I did wonder if you might have been sleepwalking. Like Anna used to." Mum searched his face worriedly. "Do you remember how you got there?

James bit his lip, not wanting to lie to her. Besides, if he was sleepwalking, they might take him to the doctor or something. Or tell people at school. What if Mum wrote a note to school, saying he might go sleepwalking during their museum trip? He thought he might die of embarrassment if Mum told Miss Morley he went sleepwalking.

"I sort of do," he said quickly. "I was really tired. I think I had a nightmare."

"You think!" Anna raised her eyebrows. "You did or you didn't?"

"Anna, don't be horrible. Things aren't always that simple." Mum frowned at her. Usually James would have made a smarmy face at Anna over Mum's shoulder, but he was too worried. That bear was making everything go wrong.

"I promise I won't do it again," he said slowly. So he'd have to sleep in his own bed again tonight.

"Now, our topic this week is all going to be based round your trip," Miss Morley explained. "Your sleepover story can be about anything to do with the night." She was pacing enthusiastically around the front of the classroom. "Bats! The moon! Nocturnal animals!"

"How long does it have to be?" Kai asked, waving at her.

Miss Morley sighed. "Why is that always the first thing you ask? Quality, not quantity, Kai!"

"But how much do we really have to write?"

"At least a side. But more would be nice. Remember to use your complex sentences, and interesting vocabulary." Miss Morley went round the room, handing out the paper and dealing with people who'd lost all their pencils, or their words, or all the ideas they'd ever had.

James sucked the end of his pencil and sighed. He enjoyed writing stories. He was usually very good at it – Miss Morley often put his work up on the wall, and he'd even won a competition in the local newspaper. But today all he could think of was the bear, and the fact that there was no way he could escape sleeping in his own room tonight. He supposed he ought to be looking forward to the sleepover more, since at least he'd be somewhere else. But he wasn't. He was convinced that the museum would be millions of shades darker than his bedroom, and full of weirdness. Besides, he wouldn't put it past that bear to travel, not at all. Now that he was sure the bear wasn't a real, actual, escaped sort of bear, that meant it was more likely to be able to find him. What if it came with him, and only he could see it? Everyone else would think he was mad.

"You need to get started, James," Miss Morley pointed out, smiling at him. "You've only got forty-five minutes."

James nodded and took his pencil out of his mouth. He supposed being afraid of the dark was to do with the night. It probably wasn't what Miss Morley was expecting, but he simply couldn't think of anything else. Was he going to write about the bear?

No. He couldn't help feeling that writing it down would only make the bear bigger and stronger – and scarier.

Maybe it could work the other way round, though? If he turned the bear into a story, perhaps it wouldn't be so frightening. And he could make the story go his way... James scowled down at his paper, and then scrawled "The Night Bear" across the top. There. Now it was only a story. He scribbled down what had happened – that he had woken up from a nightmare and found that he had slipped into another, darker and far more frightening, because it was real, and only he knew about it. As Miss Morley told them to stop, he was describing the night bear stalking out from behind the wardrobe, jaws dripping, and its eyes burning in the darkness. It was coming to eat him. Not him. The boy in the bed.

James put his pencil down with a shiver.

That wasn't what was supposed to happen. He'd been going to make the bear fall over, or turn it pink, or just make it disappear, so that it wasn't frightening any more. But it had all gone wrong – he wasn't even sure what he'd written. It was as if the bear had taken over.

"Oh, this is excellent, James!" He hadn't realized that Miss Morley was reading over his shoulder. "I'm so pleased. I thought you weren't going to get much done; you looked as though you were daydreaming. Wonderful descriptive language, well done!"

And she walked up to the front of the classroom, taking his story with her. James felt like running after her and snatching it back. The story felt as though it had been a dream, carrying him along with it – he'd hardly had to think while he was writing it down. He wasn't even sure what he had written. But he knew he didn't want Miss Morley reading it out, not to the whole class. He couldn't stop her, though.

"This is just the sort of descriptive language I was talking about, 4M. James has written about nightmares – such a good way to take the night theme!"

As she started to read, James stared down at the table, his cheeks burning. The story was good – he knew it was. It was too good. It all sounded too real. Everyone would know that the boy in the story was him. Out of the corner of his eye, he could see Kai and Freddy nudging each other and smirking. They'd be having a go at him at break time, he could tell. He closed his eyes in horror as Miss Morley lowered her voice dramatically, describing him burying his head under the duvet. Had he actually been careless enough to write that down?

One of the boys gave a muffled snort, and James glanced up for a second. It was probably Freddy. It sounded like Freddy. He wasn't scared of anything.

On the other side of his table, Elise stared at James seriously. She gave him a little grave nod. James wasn't quite sure what it meant. Well done, maybe. Or, Yes, that's just what it's like. Or perhaps, They'll all be after you now.

James sighed. It was no wonder she liked it. His story probably meant that Elise would get left alone in the playground for once. They'd got someone new and interesting to pick on instead.

"Brilliant, James, well done." Miss Morley laid his sheet of paper back down in front of him. She was smiling like she didn't know what she'd done. As though she expected him to be pleased. James smiled back at her, stretching his lips across his teeth. It wasn't really her fault.

James blundered out into the bright sun of the playground, half blind for a second in the light. There was a jostling crowd of boys around him, carrying him along.

"Grrr!" Freddy loomed up beside him, lips curled up over his teeth and his fingers curled into claws. He looked mad, but everyone was laughing.

James blinked at Freddy, and Freddy's growl

dissolved into snorting laughter. "It's all right, James, it isn't dark."

"Don't know what you're talking about." He knew he sounded feeble, but he didn't care.

"The bear won't get you."

James shrugged. It was very hard to do on purpose, and he had a feeling it didn't look natural. His shoulders went up round his ears. "It was just a story, Freddy. Don't you know what that is? It means it's made up."

Evan sniggered and nudged James with his elbow, and for a moment James felt better – he was being funny. It was going to be all right.

Freddy flushed angrily. "Didn't sound made up, James. You're scared of the dark."

"Don't be stupid."

"You're stupid. You're as stupid as Elise. Crybaby."

Elise was there too, James realized suddenly. She was behind them, coming out into the playground. She could hear what they were saying.

He ought to say that she wasn't stupid at all. He could tell Freddy he was a bully for picking on her, and he was just lucky that he wasn't scared of things. He ought to do that, and then walk over to Elise and ask if she wanted to go to the library and read, or something. James could feel the words lining up, ready to say, but he didn't say them.

"I'm nothing like her." He watched Elise's face go blank, and felt ashamed and relieved at the same time. "Are we going to play football, then?"

Freddy eyed him and glanced at Elise –
turning away, head down – and then nodded.
"Yeah. All right. Come on!" They all charged
after him, and James followed. He only looked
back for a moment, to see Elise whisking round
the corner of the playground wall to hide.

5

That night, James couldn't sleep because he felt miserable, and guilty, as well as scared of the bear. In fact, it was mostly the blank, unsurprised look on Elise's face that kept him awake. He lay there wishing that he hadn't been so mean, and knowing that he'd never be brave enough to say that, yes, he was scared of the dark. And that didn't mean there was anything wrong with him.

Actually, he did think there was, though. He was so scared of a bear that he'd probably made up that he couldn't even sleep in his own bed! But just because he knew it was silly, it didn't make the bear go away. James could see it lurking by the door, the strange light patches on its fur gleaming in the moonlight through the window. It kept shifting, too, as if it was moving from foot to foot. It had strange patchy fur, half dark and half light. The huge paws were all dark, though. If he looked closer, the moonlight would probably make its black claws glint too. He didn't look.

If only he hadn't gone and slept under Anna's bed, he probably could have got away with leaving his light on. But Mum had come and checked on him and turned it off – and then she'd checked on him again, and told him he should keep it off; he needed to go to sleep.

James curled down in his bed, pressing his head against the wall to stifle the sound of his crying. He didn't want the bear to hear him. It hadn't come right out from behind the wardrobe yet, but he had a horrible feeling that it was working up to it.

He snuffled miserably into the wall, pressed so close against it that when his bedroom door suddenly opened, he jumped.

"What are you crying for?" Anna demanded crossly, thumping down on the end of his bed.

James sat up, glaring at her resentfully. She was supposed to have come in like this two nights ago and sorted everything out. He wasn't sure he wanted her now. She'd laugh.

But then – with Anna on the end of the bed, he couldn't see the bear.

"And don't say you weren't crying, because I heard you. Grizzling on and on and on."

"Ssshhh. You'll wake up Mum and Dad."

"No, I won't. I shut the door. What's the matter?"

He felt her lean back against his wall. She was settling in to listen, then. Maybe it would be all right.

"Do you like bears?" he asked her cautiously.

"Bears?" Anna sounded honestly confused. James supposed maybe it was an odd question. Anna had probably expected him to say that he'd argued with someone at school. Or he'd been told off. Not to ask weird questions about bears.

"Do you like them?" James asked earnestly.

"Um. Yes?"

He sighed. "I thought you probably did."

"What's wrong with liking bears? Are you

asleep again? Mum said she thought you might be sleepwalking." She leaned over, staring into his eyes, as though she was trying to tell if he was actually asleep.

"No, I'm awake." James sighed. "There's a bear down the side of my wardrobe and I can't make it go away."

"You are asleep."

"I'm really not. I keep seeing it, Anna. Ever since Sunday night. It's so scary. It's massively big and it's got huge long claws and soon it's going to come out and eat me!"

"If it's that big, it wouldn't fit down the side of your wardrobe," Anna pointed out matter-of-factly.

"It can squish," James told her unhappily. "It's like a ghost bear. It can probably go as thin as paper if it wants to. It only comes out in the dark. I sort of know that it isn't real – although I did think it was at first, for about a second. I thought maybe it escaped from a zoo. But if it isn't real, that just makes it worse. No one can catch it or make it go away."

"You're just imagining it." Anna sighed in a very older-sister sort of way. "Stop being silly and go to sleep."

"I can't. It's there watching me. What if it gets bored and decides to eat me?"

"I don't think ghosts can eat people," Anna said thoughtfully. "Actually, I don't think ghosts exist." But she didn't sound certain at all.

"I can see it," James told her wearily. "I've been seeing it all week."

"Oh, so that's why you were sleeping under

my bed?" Anna looked slightly guilty. "Sorry I said you were being creepy, then."

"It was because I forgot you were at swimming," James explained. "I wanted to sleep at the end of your bed, but I thought you'd kick me out when you got back, so I slept under the bed instead."

"You are so weird," Anna muttered.

"Please make it go away, Anna."

"If it's your ghost, you'll have to get rid of it," Anna said, rather unhelpfully. "How can I make it go away if I can't even see it?"

"You can't see it at all?" James peered round her at the bear, and it loomed back at him. He shuddered.

"There's nothing there." Anna leaned closer to him, peering at his face in the darkness. Her eyes were adjusting now, and she could see how scared he looked. "You really do think there's a bear, don't you?" She sat back against the wall again, thinking. "Are you sure it's a mean bear?" she asked at last.

"Yes!"

"So, what does it look like?"

"It's really big – really, really big. And it's got black-and-white patches."

"You mean it's a panda?" Anna asked doubtfully.

"Um. Maybe."

James could almost hear Anna rolling her eyes. "You do know what a panda looks like, don't you? Sort of big and cuddly and black and white?"

"This one isn't cuddly," James muttered.

"But if it's black and white, it's a panda. Oh, stay there. I'll show you."

James felt his bed bounce as Anna sprang up and darted out of the room. He opened his mouth to tell her to watch out for the bear, but she was already gone. The bear seemed to be surprised by her dashing past too. It reeled back, teetering, as though she'd swiped it in the stomach on the way past.

He could hear her rustling and thumping in her bedroom, and then she was back, flicking on the light. James gasped as the room went white, and looked eagerly at the side of his wardrobe, wondering if he'd see the bear dart back out of the light. But there was only his dressing gown, hanging on the hook beside the door. He'd been too slow.

"Look." Anna laid her iPad out on the bed between them and swiped down the screen to show him a stream of photos. "There, you see. Pandas. Big black-and-white bears. They aren't fierce, James, they're really cute."

James looked suspiciously down at the screen. The bears were cute – round-faced and sort of cuddly-looking. But they were big – massive, actually. They looked like they could knock out a boy with one wave of a paw.

"Look at the little baby one!" Anna said, giggling at the smallest bear's teddy-bear ears. "Ooooh, there's a video from this zoo. Look! So cute! How can you be scared of a little baby bear like that?"

"The one behind my wardrobe isn't a little baby one," James hissed. "They don't look like

the one behind my wardrobe. Anna, it's huge.
And anyway, they might be cute, but they've still
got teeth."

"James, they live on bamboo," Anna sighed.
"It says so here, look. And they're endangered.
There's only about two thousand of them left in
the wild."

"Bamboo?" James looked down at the screen

doubtfully. Bamboo was what Dad's garden sticks for holding up his bean plants were made of. "They eat wood?"

"It's like a big grass before it dries out. But I don't think it's very exciting for them, nothing but bamboo." Anna giggled. "And they have to eat so much of it that they poo forty times a day!"

"What? I don't believe you." James read where she was pointing. "That's mad."

"Pandas are mad," Anna said firmly. "They don't do anything except eat; they have to eat all the time just to keep going." She put an arm around his shoulders. "No panda has got time to be sitting behind your wardrobe trying to scare you to death. They don't even walk very far; they haven't got the energy."

James looked at the cuddly bears in the

photos and tried to fit them together with the hulking creature in the corner of his room. Vegetarian, slow, sweet bears. And hardly any of them left. Maybe he shouldn't have been so scared.

But he still wished the bear would go away.

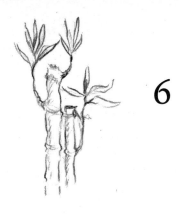

6

James woke up all at once. It was like turning on a light switch – he'd been asleep, and then suddenly, he was wide awake. Something had moved in his room.

He lay there, staring into the darkness, wondering how he knew. Had he heard a noise? It was almost as if he'd felt the movement – like a shifting in the air. James's eyes began to adjust to the darkness, and he peered cautiously over to the space beside the wardrobe, looking for the bear.

He had hoped that it might go away after Anna had shown him the photos the night before. He'd even looked up more information on pandas during his IT class at school that morning. They were supposed to be researching wild animals, ready for their trip to the museum the next day. James had seen a lot more cute baby panda videos, and he was starting to agree with Anna that pandas were nice to look at. But on the other hand, he now knew that pandas had cute round faces because of the muscles they'd built up eating all that bamboo. He'd pointed this out to Anna at dinner time, but she said it didn't matter. They were still cute and snuggly and not great fierce monsters that he needed to be scared of. James wasn't convinced at all. They had the claws – and the teeth, and the super-powerful bamboo-chewing jaw muscles. A panda could definitely chomp him into little bits, even if it would probably spit him out afterwards because he didn't taste like bamboo.

He'd lain in bed thinking about it, though, and he'd fallen asleep feeling quite hopeful. Surely now he knew all these facts about pandas – now he knew that he could definitely run faster than a panda, that he could probably hop faster than a panda – surely that ought to mean he wasn't scared of the panda in his bedroom any more. It shouldn't be there. If he wasn't scared of it, it ought to fizzle away to nothing. It should disappear.

It hadn't.

It was leaning out from the side of the wardrobe, gazing at him. James swallowed sickly, his fingers gripping the duvet so tight that he thought it might tear. Until now, the bear had stood still. It had seemed to be looking in his direction, but he'd never thought it was staring at him. Now it looked curious. It was something about the tilt of the creature's head.

James stared back. Then he swallowed again, and coughed a little, and said, "You're not real." His voice came out thin and breathy, and too feeble to convince anyone. He coughed firmly and said, louder this time, "You're not real. I don't know if you're a dream, or a nightmare, or maybe a ghost, but you're not real and I don't believe in you."

Nothing happened. Except that the panda leaned a little closer – as though it was intrigued. The dark patches round its eyes made it look confused.

"That means you have to go away."

This time the panda leaned further out, so far that it had to step forward so as not to fall over. It lumbered into the middle of James's bedroom floor, and just about avoided stepping on a large Lego spaceship.

"I don't believe in you! I don't believe in you!" James squeaked.

The panda lifted its massive back paws carefully to step around the Lego – it was better at that than James's mum was – and stomped towards his bed, its front paws swinging by its sides.

James scuttled backwards, flinging himself into the corner of his bed by the wall, and tried to scream. It was coming to eat him! Mum and Dad and Anna would definitely be able to see it now, wouldn't they?

But the scream stuck in his throat. He just couldn't make a noise with the huge creature leaning over him. The fur of its paw brushed across his arm, thick and harsh, and James couldn't breathe. The air was stuck in his throat, and the sharp, strong smell of a bear rolled over him. James closed his eyes, waiting to feel the teeth or the claws. He wasn't sure how it would start eating him. Head first?

Then the warmth of the great furry body drew away, and James heard the soft thumping of its steps across the room. He opened his eyes a fraction, still expecting to see huge, bamboo-sharpened teeth just millimetres away. But the panda was sniffing thoughtfully at his bookcase, as though it fancied sitting down with a book.

"What are you doing?" James asked waveringly. "Why are you even here?"

The panda turned back to look at him, and James cursed himself inside. He should have got up and run as soon as it wasn't looking at him! Why on earth did he have to go and ask it questions?

The bear picked its way carefully back, and then sat down on James's bedside table with a juddering thump. It sat on its bottom with its back paws on the floor, just like a human would. Or a teddy bear. Its front paws dangled over its tummy, and it stared at James, looking rather foolish. James's clock wobbled on the edge of the table, and then fell off. The panda watched it go, and then looked back at James apologetically.

"Can you talk?" James asked suddenly. A

talking panda wasn't any stranger than a panda in his bedroom, was it?

The panda didn't say anything. It just stared at him, rather hopefully.

"Probably not," James muttered. "I don't think you have the right-shaped mouth for talking. Although you're not real anyway, so if you wanted to talk you probably could, you know."

The panda shifted, and the bedside table creaked and wobbled under its weight. It let out a long, heavy sigh, and gazed at James dolefully. The black patches around its eyes gave it a mournful look.

"Are you lost?" James asked suddenly. It was rather a shock to think about the bear like that, after four nights of thinking it was a ravening monster that wanted to eat him, but he couldn't help it. The panda looked sad. It felt sad – a huge lump of sad black-and-white fur. It was actually making James feel quite sad too. Maybe he'd gone from having a scary bear in his bedroom to a miserable one. James let out his breath in a shaky whoosh. At least it really didn't seem to want to eat him. It wasn't going to be any easier to get back to sleep, though.

The panda looked smaller now that it was sitting on his bedside table, and its shoulders were hunched over. "Are you lonely?" James whispered. "Is that why you come and sit in my room?" He sat up a bit, leaning towards the bear. "You do look lonely."

It sniffed.

"I know how you feel," James muttered.

"School's really weird at the moment. Everyone's just obsessed with getting Kai and Freddy to like them and we all have to play whatever game they say." He glanced resentfully at the panda. "You can't put a foot wrong, or they say you can't be in the game, and then no one talks to you all lunchtime. And you nearly got me in trouble because I wrote about you. I had to swear the story wasn't about me and I'd just made it all up, or they'd all have thought I was a baby because I'm scared of the dark."

The panda didn't say anything, but James could tell it was listening. It leaned closer, so he could feel the warmth of its fur.

"There's a girl called Elise in my class and she's scared of the dark too. She's scared of a lot of things, actually. Dogs and spiders and jumping in the swimming pool. All the boys say she's such a baby. If they find out I'm scared of the dark too, they'll say I'm just like her." He hunched his arms around his knees. "She's quite nice, though. I'd never talked to her much before Monday." He glanced over at the panda uncomfortably. "I teased her like the others did." He was silent for a minute. "I wish I hadn't. I said mean stuff

about her. Because if I didn't, Freddy and the others would have been mean to me." He looked anxiously at the bear. "You understand, don't you?" he added, putting out one hand and laying it on top of the nearest mighty paw. "I don't want to be all on my own. Like Elise. And you."

The panda didn't say anything. It just breathed, in and out, slow and deep, and James slept, with his hand on the bear's heavy paw.

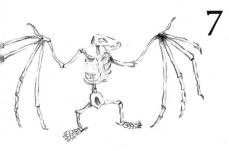

7

No one was paying very much attention to Miss Morley. It was too hard not to keep looking over at the side of the classroom, at the tables where all their project work – Viking ships and models of the Colosseum, or Egyptian death masks – was piled up. Stacked neatly underneath them were rucksacks and sleeping bags, with cuddly toys stuffed in at the top. Miss Morley had said that everyone should bring a bear, which was clever of her, James thought. It meant that no one would look silly for bringing one if they really couldn't sleep without it. He'd had to dig an old toy dog out of the bottom of his wardrobe – he wasn't that much into soft toys any more. Certainly not bears.

James blinked to himself thoughtfully. Did he really think that now? He wasn't sure. Two nights ago he would have done anything to get rid of the bear, but now he was wondering what it would be like, going to sleep somewhere else – somewhere with no huge furry sentinel. If he woke up in the night at the museum, he'd be all alone in the dark.

His fingers tightened on his pencil, and he stared down at his book, confused. Was that truly what he thought the panda was now? A guard? Someone who watched over him? He twisted the pencil round in his hand. He had been so scared! He'd run to hide under Anna's bed, desperate to escape from the monster in his room! How could he suddenly like the bear?

He did, though. He was actually going to miss it.

The museum was very big, and there were a lot of things in it. Mostly quite cool things – even a real Egyptian mummy with an X-ray, so you could see the bones inside – but they had trailed through twenty-three different galleries, and Miss Morley seemed to think it was important to listen in all of them. James's feet were hurting. He was so tired from standing up and listening that he couldn't even imagine not being able to sleep, but he was still worried he might wake up in the middle of the night. He'd also had to keep trying not to get anywhere near

Kai and Freddy when they were gathered round fossils or bat skeletons or the incredibly creepy anaconda skin, so as not to get told off when they started messing around. It was quite tricky, managing that without looking as though he didn't want to be next to Freddy and Kai, which would instantly make him not part of the gang.

He was on the edge of the gang as they laid out their sleeping bags and settled down, chatting. He sort of had to be there, even though he was pretty sure that they'd smuggled in a load of sweets, and they were probably going to get into trouble. Miss Morley had said in her fiercest voice that there was absolutely no eating in the galleries whatsoever, under any circumstances, full stop. But that hadn't stopped Freddy and his mates. James could hear the rustling noises coming from Kai's sleeping bag right now.

James wished he and Evan could just edge a bit further away. But Evan loved football, and there was no way he was going to risk getting left out of Kai and Freddy's lunchtime matches. Evan was practically asleep, though, curled up on the other side of Kai. James was stuck with them all.

"There's a space here, Elise, look. Hello, James." Miss Morley was standing right next to him, and Kai had suddenly frozen, looking guilty, with one cheek swollen full of Haribo. "Can you edge that way a bit, to make some more room for Elise?"

James nodded, and wriggled over obediently. Elise was standing behind Miss Morley in her pyjamas, her arms full of unrolled sleeping bag. She was very pale – even paler than usual.

"There. You'll be fine," Miss Morley said, smiling. "I'll come and check on you again in a minute. I just need to sort what's going on under the dinosaur skeleton." She hurried away looking grim, and Elise laid her sleeping bag down next to James and burrowed into it, right up to her nose.

"What happened?" James whispered, too curious to care that the other boys were muttering crossly about Elise nicking their floor, and bringing Miss Morley too close. Kai was pretending to choke on his Haribo.

"Alice bought a toy spider in the museum shop," Elise whispered faintly. "She put it in my rucksack. It was on my toothbrush."

"Oh."

"I haven't cleaned my teeth." Elise sounded like she might cry.

"That's OK." James eyed her worriedly. He wasn't sure what he would do if she really did cry. Run for Miss Morley, probably. But he felt guilty about being mean to her the other day, and he wanted to make up for it. He was sick of the other boys being cruel, and making him cruel too, and now they'd all shifted their sleeping bags round so they had their backs to her. None of them would notice if he whispered.

"It won't do anything to your teeth if you don't clean them for one night," he promised. "I skip cleaning them sometimes in the morning, if I'm in a rush, and last time I went to the dentist, she said my teeth were perfect."

Elise nodded, and then looked at him sideways with a very small smile. "I'm not sitting next to you in the mornings any more, then."

James sniggered quietly.

"Are you scared of the dark?" Elise whispered, pulling the hood of her sleeping bag tighter round her head. She looked like the little model Inuit baby in the display in gallery number James-wasn't-sure-but-it-felt-like-ten-thousand-and-something.

"No!" he whispered back fiercely.

"Oh. . . I just wondered if you might be," Elise added. "Because you looked worried whenever Miss Morley was talking about the trip. And then you wrote that story about the night bear."

"I made that up!" James hissed back. "Why doesn't anybody get that?"

Elise eyed him from deep inside of her sleeping bag. "It was too good to be all made up. It was right. Nobody understands being scared like that unless they actually have been."

James stared at her. Elise's voice was still shaky, and she'd pulled the sleeping bag even tighter, so that only a tiny circle of her face was open to the darkness of the night. She was worse than he was, he realized, feeling slightly proud of himself.

"It's a panda," he muttered.

"Have you had it a long time?" Elise asked. She made it sound like a pet.

"No... Only a few days. I don't know why it suddenly turned up. But I'm sort of getting used to it now."

Elise shuddered. "Lucky."

"What's yours, then?" James asked, leaning over on one elbow to stare curiously at her.

"Not an animal." Elise sighed. "It's just the dark. I don't like it touching me."

James swallowed hard. That was exactly how he'd felt sometimes. As if the dark was a feeling, thick and sticky and smothering. He thought hard, trying to work out something helpful to say, but he couldn't. It was no good telling her that the dark couldn't really touch her at all. He was willing to bet that lots of people had told her that, and it hadn't helped.

"When I go to sleep, I'll turn over so I'm all covered in the sleeping bag," Elise explained.

"Good plan. Don't the lights help?" The gallery ceiling was covered in tiny lights, laid out

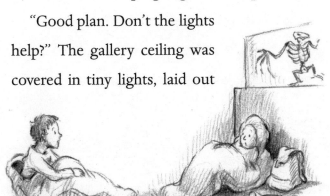

in patterns like the stars in the night sky. Even in the daytime, the main lights were turned off at certain times, so people could see them. James vaguely recognized one or two, but his road was in the middle of the town, and the street lights made the stars hard to see.

"Not much. I've got a torch, though, for if I get really scared. I can put it on inside the sleeping bag, so Miss Morley doesn't see."

"What are you talking to her for?"

James jumped as someone grabbed his shoulder. Freddy was leaning over him, smirking.

"I wasn't!" he snapped back. And then, because Freddy's fingers had dug in, and because he was tired, and sick of running around doing what Freddy and Kai wanted all the time, he said, "Just mind your own business."

"James and Elise, sitting in a tree. . ." Freddy began to chant, and James rolled his eyes. Couldn't he think of anything better than that?

"Shut up, or I'll tell about all those sweets in the front pocket of your rucksack," he growled.

"You do and me and Kai'll get you."

"Yeah, I'm really scared," James muttered, even though he actually was. He might have to go and hang around where the lunch ladies were so he was safe. He'd never get to play football any more, he thought miserably. Evan would stop being mates with him. Freddy caterpillar-scrunched himself back over to the other boys, huddled inside his sleeping bag, whispering and shooting black looks at James and Elise.

"That was a crazy thing to do!" Elise breathed at him, round-eyed.

"Thanks a lot!" James lay back down with a thud that hurt his head. He'd been sticking up for her, couldn't she at least see that? And why didn't she just go to sleep? He could feel her staring at him.

"Sorry. . ." she whispered eventually.

James humped up one shoulder away from her and heard her sigh, but she didn't go on trying to get him to say it was OK, like most people would have done. Anna wouldn't have shut up about it.

He lay there for a while, trying to feel cross with her, and instead feeling mean again. Then he turned back over, and had to wriggle about in his sleeping bag to get it the right way up again.

That made enough noise and fussing for her to look at him.

"You all right?" he muttered.

"Yes, except I can't sleep." She sighed and sat up a little, looking out at the others.

"Me neither."

"I think everyone else is. Except Miss Morley and Mrs Barker. They're over by the toilets and I can hear them whispering. Are you worried your panda's going to come?"

James tested himself thoughtfully, trying to see what he was worried about. He was sure it wasn't that. "No. I almost like him," he admitted, sounding a little surprised. "I didn't know I would."

There was a sudden, strangled gulp nearby, and a sleeping bag thrashed as someone fought

95

their way out. A pale face looked over at them in the darkness, and James recognized Freddy, even though his dark spiked hair was flattened with sleep. He was gasping for breath, and looked quite different, his eyes wide open in fright.

"What's the matter?" James whispered at him.

"Nothing!"

"Nightmare," Elise breathed, with an experienced look.

"Want me to get Miss Morley?" James asked.

"No!"

Freddy couldn't admit to being woken up by a bad dream, of course. That was the sort of thing Elise did.

"Elise has got a torch, if you want to borrow

it a minute?" he suggested. He saw Freddy's face twist in the half-dark with a sudden eagerness. He really wanted that torch. But then they'd know he was scared. They might tell.

"All right," he muttered at last. "Yeah, can I borrow the torch?" He glanced shiftily at Elise. "Please? Only because I've lost the sweets down the end of my sleeping bag. I just want to look for them."

Elise passed the torch to James, and James reached over to hand it to Freddy. He huddled back inside his sleeping bag, flicking it on, and James could hear his breathing, harsh and fast. The light made his face look even whiter, and he pulled the sleeping bag up around his head, just as Elise had.

Then he stuck an arm out of the sleeping

bag, and handed a couple of chocolate eclairs to James. "I'll give the torch back in a minute, all right? There's still some down here. They fell out of the bag."

Elise nodded and gave James a tiny smile. They both knew, but they'd pretend they didn't. She lay back down. "OK."

Freddy stayed crouched, sitting up inside his sleeping bag, and James moved a little closer to him, smiling sleepily in the dark. Freddy and Elise were warm on either side of him, like the panda. Maybe the panda was in his room right now. Perhaps it was wondering where he was? *I hope you're all right*, he thought to the panda as he fell asleep. *I'm coming back, don't worry.*

8

James browsed the shelves thoughtfully. He didn't have much time – Miss Morley didn't want to let them all in the museum shop at once, so each group only had ten minutes to do all their shopping. Did he have enough money to buy a present for Anna? He'd thought he might have to, given that he'd snapped at Freddy, and he'd need her to stick up for him. He quite often saw her on the way home from school, walking in a gang with her mates, and he knew his cool big sister made him look more grown up. But Freddy had offered him another chocolate eclair when he'd woken up that morning, and he hadn't said anything rude to Elise at all. So perhaps it would be all right.

He turned round to look at the shelf behind him, and felt his mouth twist into a smile. There was his panda. Standing on a shelf, looking friendly and slightly gormless. Its front paws were dangling over its fat furry stomach, just as they had been in his room. Even though it was only a plastic model, it even had the same sad black eyepatches. James seized it eagerly and hurried away to pay. Then he tucked the panda into his pocket, feeling the cool lump of it banging against his leg. It was reassuringly solid.

When he got back home, he thought, smiling a small, relieved smile to himself, he would put it on his bedside table. And the real panda could come and sit next to it.

"You look shattered, James. It's only six o'clock." Dad was gazing at him across the table. "Couldn't you get to sleep last night? Or did you stay up talking?"

James lifted his chin off his hand and tried to look awake. He'd quite enjoyed the sleepover in the end, and Evan's mum had been murmuring about Evan having a sleepover for his birthday in a few weeks' time. He didn't want to miss out just because Mum and Dad thought he looked too tired now.

"I didn't! It was only about nine when I went to sleep, and it'd have been earlier, but Freddy had a nightmare."

Mum peered at him. "Actually, you've been looking a bit tired all week. Since we lost you and you turned up under Anna's bed."

"Is it that panda still?" Anna asked interestedly, and then she sucked up a long strand of pasta with a slurp.

Mum shuddered at her manners, and then said, "What panda?"

James rolled his eyes at his sister. "Nothing, Mum. Just a weird dream I had." He noticed a worried glance between his mum and dad, and added quickly, "Honestly, I'm OK!"

"Was that why you were under Anna's bed? You had a nightmare?" Mum looked sympathetic. "A bad one?"

"Sort of..." James wriggled on his chair. He didn't want to tell Mum and Dad any more about the panda. It was his secret. Well, his and Anna's. He glanced over at Anna pleadingly. *Don't tell. . .*

Anna looked back, and then a blank, I-don't-know-anything look settled over her face. She slurped more pasta.

James's mum started to look really worried – she didn't even tell Anna off. She leaned over and put an arm round his shoulders. "Why on earth didn't you tell us that night? That you'd had a bad nightmare? You could have come and sat with us downstairs for a bit."

James shrugged against the warmth of her arm. "It was all about being afraid of the dark. It's babyish. I didn't want to say."

"Everyone's afraid of something, sweetheart."

His dad nodded. "You know what I'm afraid of?"

James shook his head, surprised. He hadn't thought his dad was scared of anything.

"Horses. Can't get anywhere near one. I start shivering and then I feel sick. Your uncle Matt tried to persuade me to stroke one once, and I threw up all over his shoes."

"Really?" James stared at him. "Why? Did a horse hurt you?"

His dad shrugged. "That's the weird thing, I don't know. I don't remember it, and your gran says she can't remember me ever being near a horse when I was little. It could be something as silly as being spooked by a horse on TV. I just don't know." He smiled at James. "I had to pretend to have a stomach bug the day my class went on a trip to the farm." He frowned to himself. "What about a night light? We could

104

go and get you one tomorrow. Wouldn't that help?"

"Maybe..." James wasn't sure if anything would make the panda go away. Or even if he wanted it gone. But a night light would be nice anyway. "Yeah, OK. A night light."

"And for tonight you can have this." Dad got up and went to the drawers in one of the kitchen cabinets, pulling out a heavy, solid sort of torch, cased in black rubber. It looked businesslike. James stroked it admiringly and clicked it on, sending out a rich orangey glow that showed against the wall even in the light. The rubbery weight of the torch would be comforting to have in bed with him, he could tell. It was like a weapon against the dark.

"Thanks, Dad!" James hugged him gratefully, the torch still gripped tightly in his hand.

The panda was there when James woke up. It was back over between the wardrobe and the door, looming down over him. James gulped. Even after their talk on Thursday night, the panda was still scarily big.

He burrowed for the torch, flailing around under his duvet, until it settled into his hands like the hilt of a sword. With a gasp of relief, he switched it on, and held it out towards the bear, the beam swooping and shuddering through the darkness. If he could see the bear better, it wouldn't look scary. He wanted it sitting on his bedside table again, like a friend, there to share the dark with him.

The orange glare was so bright that it was hard for a moment to see what was going on. But there didn't seem to be a bear – any sort of bear.

It was his dressing gown.

His white dressing gown, hanging up on a hook. That was all.

James gaped at it. Had he really worked himself up into such a state just because of his dressing gown? Now that he looked at it, he could see that of course that was all there was. It must have been something to do with the way the shadows fell. There had never been a bear, not even a ghost one? He felt so stupid, and … and disappointed. His bear had been special. It was his – and it wasn't real. Just a few folds of fabric seen in the shadows. The panda had been stolen away from him, and James felt like crying.

But – it had been there. He'd felt its fur, and its hot breath on his cheek. He'd told it about Elise, and Freddy and Kai. It had listened to him. He had turned on the torch and sent it away.

James shone the torch on to his bedside table, and the little model panda, gazing back at him.

Its black eyepatches looked sadder than ever. "Sorry. . ." he whispered. "I didn't mean to chase you away. . ."

The toy panda stared back, and James gulped and flicked off the torch. The darkness rushed back, thick and choking, and for a moment he huddled down under its weight. Then he sat up straighter again, and looked over towards the door.

There was still no panda. It was only his dressing gown, of course. Somehow he couldn't see it as a panda any more, even though he tried. Perhaps it couldn't come back, now he knew it wasn't really there. He'd sent it away.

James flung himself down against his pillow miserably. It was too late. Why couldn't he have realized before?

He pressed his cheek into the hot cotton of his pillowcase and sniffed, so loudly that he almost didn't hear the creaking of the floor as heavy paws crept over it. But he felt the end of his bed rock, and then settle, as a plump panda sat down.

Then the gentle weight of a paw, resting on his back, and the soft, pleased sighing of its breath.

Look out for more by
HOLLY WEBB

A
Cat Called
PENGUIN

HOLLY WEBB

Illustrated by Polly Dunbar

The
CHOCOLATE
Dog

HOLLY WEBB

Illustrated by Sharon Rentta

LOOKING
for Bear

HOLLY WEBB

Illustrated by Helen Stephens

A TiGER Tale

HOLLY WEBB

Illustrated by Catherine Rayner

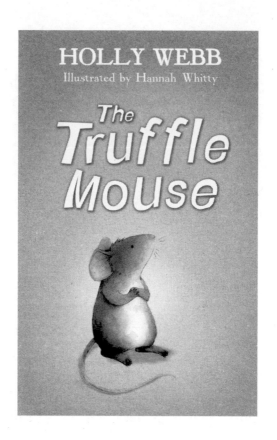

HOLLY WEBB
Illustrated by Hannah Whitty

The Truffle Mouse

Read on for a sneak peek of

The Truffle Mouse

"Can we go?" Alice stood next to her mum, with her coat on, eyeing the empty plate. "You said after lunch. You *have* finished."

"Actually, I was thinking of having an apple…" But her mum was only teasing, Alice could tell. "Yes. All right. You've been very patient, actually. Where were you all morning? I thought you'd be hanging around in here begging to have lunch at half-past ten."

Alice handed her a fistful of papers, covered in drawings. "I was doing these," she explained. They were covered in tiny, delicate drawings, in her newest felt tips, the ones Dad had given her the weekend before. "It's a list, do you see?" she explained to her mum. "All the things a hamster needs."

"Really? All of this?" her mum murmured, turning the pages round to peer at the edges – the paper was covered. "I thought a hamster just needed a cage. And food. Alice, this isn't a cage!" She pointed to a lacy-looking pink and purple building. "It's a hamster *palace*! There's a flag on top of it!"

"I know." Alice leaned over it admiringly. "It would be so cool to have a hamster cage with towers… There's an under-the-sea one on the other side. And that's a space hamster ship." She patted her mum's shoulder. "It's all right, Mum, I know there won't be a hamster palace at the pet shop. I was just getting excited, that's all. I've been looking forward to this weekend so much. The week was so long, it felt like it was going on for ever. Especially school." She made a face. "I know it'll just be a cage. Although, actually, when I looked online, one of the pet websites had a cage that did look sort of spaceship-like – all coloured tubes for the hamster to climb through – it's really cool. Lucy's hamster has a cage a bit like that too, just not as many bits sticking out." Lucy was Alice's best friend from school; she'd been given a hamster for her birthday, a couple of months before. Alice riffled to the back of the stack of papers and showed her mum a page she'd printed.

Her mum frowned a little, turning the paper sideways. "It does look very smart. Does it, ummm, does it keep them in?"

Alice blinked at her, not sure what she meant.

"I mean, the hamster can't get out?" her mum asked worriedly. "All those tubes. It looks a bit fragile. The hamster wouldn't be able to escape?"

Alice leaned against her shoulder. "How can you be scared of a hamster?" she giggled. "They're *tiny*."

Her mum sighed. "I'm not really scared, I just don't want to go into your bedroom and find a hamster asleep in your washing basket, or something like that. I've never had a little pet, you know that. Only cats. I'm sure I'll love a hamster once I get used to it, though," she added quickly.

*

Alice wasn't sure her mum would get used to a hamster. She was trying to cheer up Alice by buying her one. It was because Ms Hickman, Alice's teacher, had told Mum and Dad at Parents' Evening earlier on that week that Alice "sometimes seemed a little sad" and "was very quiet this week". Alice knew exactly what she'd said because she'd been waiting outside in the hallway at school and Mum and Dad had discussed it in hissing whispers all the way back to their cars. They hadn't thought Alice was listening, but of course she was.

Alice didn't realize she was any quieter than usual. It was odd. She supposed Ms Hickman would notice, though. It made her wonder what her teachers had said about her before.

Mum always just came home from Parents' Evening and said that it was fine, but she needed to be neater with her handwriting, or something like that.

Mum and Dad would never have let her hear them saying that kind of thing before, but they were so cross with each other that it seemed as though they'd forgotten Alice was there. Which was funny when it was her they were talking about. She'd felt like joining in, and saying of course she was sad. What did they expect? They'd sold her lovely house, the house she'd always lived in, with her own proper bedroom. And now she had to get used to two new not-so-nice houses, and nothing was ever in the right place when she wanted it. And now there was Tilly. Her dad was going to be somebody else's dad too. Wasn't she allowed to be sad? Weren't *they* sad about what had happened?

Alice wasn't sure. Maybe Dad wasn't sad at all.

Alice gathered up her drawings of hamster cages carefully and gave her mum a quick one-armed hug. She didn't understand how anybody could not want a hamster in their house – they were so soft! And the little black eyes, like beads! But she knew that Mum didn't, really didn't. She was only doing it to make Alice happy.

"I can't believe we're going to the pet shop today," she murmured. "I've wanted a hamster for so long."

"Last week you said we ought to get a Shetland Pony," her mum pointed out.

Alice hugged her tighter. "I know. I didn't really mean it, though. You made a face when I was talking about what colour hamster I'd like to get. So I thought I'd better make you grateful I was starting with a small animal."

"Very clever." Her mum snorted. "Cunning. And don't think that starting off small with a hamster means I'll let you get something else bigger in a few months. A hamster. One hamster. That's it. Poor Tiger's already going to think you don't love him any more."

Alice did love Tiger, of course she did. But he was Mum's cat – he adored Mum, and he always wanted to sit on her lap. He only sat on Alice if she'd got to her mum's lap first, and then she was just a sort of cushion that had got in the way... Tiger didn't mind if Alice picked him up, but he'd only keep still for about ten seconds, then he would wriggle firmly away. A hamster would be *hers*.

Alice smiled sweetly. "Yes, Mum." She hauled her mum up out of the chair, and whisked her plate over to the sink. Then she scooped up her mum's handbag and the car keys, pressing them into her arms.

"I might need the loo..." her mum muttered.

Alice glared at her. "If I did that, you'd say I was being *deliberately difficult*. Please let's go!"

Her mum planted a kiss on the top of Alice's tangled brown hair – she'd been running her fingers through it while she was drawing.

"I'm ready really. Come on. It'll only take ten minutes to get there."

Alice gave her a sudden, panicked look. "What if they don't have any hamsters?" she asked, frozen in the middle of the kitchen. "I didn't think of that."

"They do, I phoned them the other day to check," her mum said calmly. "They said they always have several and not to worry."

"Oh..." Alice breathed in shakily. "OK. Thanks, Mum. I'm just so excited. It would be awful if we couldn't get a hamster today."

"Alice, it wouldn't be the end of the world." Her mum eyed her worriedly. "You do know the hamster might not be all that friendly to start with, don't you? You won't be upset if it doesn't want to be cuddled?"

"No." Alice followed her out to the car. "I won't, I promise." She thought about it for the whole drive, though. What if the hamster just didn't like her? Sometimes people just didn't like each other. There were a couple of people at school who didn't like *her*, even though she'd never even looked at them the wrong way. What if she never made friends with it? That would be almost worse than no hamster at all. . .

The pet shop cheered her up though – it was lovely. Alice had been there a couple of times before when she'd persuaded Dad to let her go in and look when they were on the way to the hardware shop down the road. The man in the shop didn't mind if you didn't actually buy anything. Alice guessed he was used to people coming in to coo over the hamsters and the guinea pigs. Last time there had been a gorgeous grey rabbit, with soft, floppy ears. But Mum had said no to rabbits when she'd asked before. Too much work, and their new garden was mostly patio. Alice had bought a book on hamsters instead, and told the man that one of these days she was coming back to buy the real thing.

He smiled at her from behind the counter as she peered round the door. "The hamster girl!"

Alice beamed at him. "I'm actually allowed to buy one today," she told him, grinning. "And the cage, and everything."

"You know where they are." He waved her towards the back of the shop, which was covered in a wall of cages. "There's a lovely cinnamon girl and a cream long-haired. Lot of work grooming him, though – you might not want to be doing that with your first hamster."

"Long-haired?" Mum stared down the aisle towards the cages. "I thought – well, I thought a hamster was a hamster, to be honest. . ."

The pet shop man grinned at her. "Syrian, Dwarf, Russian, Roborovski . . . short-haired, long-haired, Rex and Satin." He shook his head at Alice's mum, who was gazing at him in horror. "Don't worry, I'm only teasing you. All ours are short-haired apart from that cream male. And I wouldn't recommend the smaller breeds for you – too wriggly and fast. You want a nice, cuddly Syrian for a first pet."

"Yes..." Alice's mum agreed, a little doubtfully.

Alice caught her hand and pulled her down the aisle to look in the cages. Most of the hamsters were dozing in the little bedrooms, half hidden by piles of litter, or fluffy bedding. "Oh, they're all plump and snuggly!" Alice whispered. "Look at the lovely reddish one! And this one's got spots!"

"Cute," her mum agreed. "He looks like a tortoiseshell cat. He's really unusual, isn't he? I didn't know hamsters came in all those colours."

"Or a little bear." Alice pressed closer to the cage, watching the grey and peach hamster lumber determinedly through the woody stuff on the floor to his food bowl. "He's so funny!"

"So, would you like him?" Alice's mum was trying to sound cheerful and enthusiastic. "I'll go and look at the cages."

"Maybe," Alice murmured back. "Have we seen all of them?" She peered into the cage at the end of the row. "Is there another hamster in here? Oh, look, he's chocolate-coloured, Mum! I can see a bit of his fur under the bedding." She looked round to point the hamster out to her mum, but she'd moved up the aisle to look at all the stuff that they'd need.

The cotton wool bedding shifted a little, as if the creature underneath had heard her notice him. A pinkish-brown nose edged out from under the pile, fringed with delicate silvery whiskers. Alice caught just a glimpse of a shining dark eye. The hamster was watching her. The others hadn't seemed to notice that she and her mum were there – or, at least, they hadn't been all that interested. This one was eyeing her curiously – Alice only wished she could see him too. Or her. She couldn't tell from just a nose and an eye – her hamster book had said that actually it was quite tricky to see the difference, however carefully you looked.

"Come on out and see me," she whispered to the dark-eyed face. "Maybe you're one of those small hamsters that the man was talking about – you don't look quite the same as those big ones. Not from the bits of you I can see, anyway." The little nose twitched and then came out a little further, and Alice smiled.

She wished the man from the shop hadn't said dwarf hamsters were too wriggly. This one was so sweet. Perhaps she could convince the man that she'd be careful?

And then the little dark face came right out from underneath the bedding and stared at her, and Alice stared back.

Not a hamster at all – a tiny, chocolate-brown ball of a mouse.

HOLLY has always loved animals. As a child she had two dogs, a cat, and at one point, nine gerbils (an accident). Holly's other love is books. Holly now lives in Reading with her husband, three sons and three very spoilt cats.